The
Christmas Garland

By **Lisa Flinn** and **Barbara Younger**   *Illustrated by* **Lucy Corvino**

The Christmas Garland

ideals children's books
Nashville, Tennessee

ISBN 0-8249-5460-2

Published by Ideals Children's Books
An imprint of Ideals Publications
A division of Guideposts
535 Metroplex Drive, Suite 250
Nashville, Tennessee 37211
www.idealsbooks.com

Color separations by Precision Color Graphics, Franklin, Wisconsin

Printed and Bound in Italy

Library of Congress CIP data on file

10 9 8 7 6 5 4 3 2 1

Book design by Eve DeGrie

For our mothers, who taught us the crafts
of Christmas, and for our children,
who will keep the traditions.
—LF, BY

In the Holy Land, a fragrant grass grows wild in the fields. When dry, this flowering grass becomes a sweet-smelling bedstraw once used in mattresses and stables. The grass is called *Galium verum*.

One night long ago, all of the flowers of the *Galium verum* turned from white to gold. . . .

Pass it over, tuck it under, pass it over, tuck it under."

"Hannah! Where are you and where is the bedstraw?"

At her father's call, Hannah stopped braiding the straw, jumped up, and placed the flowered garland around her neck. Gathering an armful of the straw, she hurried back to the shepherds' camp.

The winter sun cast long shadows over the flock of sheep as Hannah spread the straw on the ground. She made two beds, then laid blankets over the straw.

While Hannah's father cooked supper, she started to work on her garland again. The small white clusters of flowers on each stalk reminded her of her mother, who had died in the spring. Hannah's mother had taught her daughter how to braid the flowers of the field.

One of the sheep came up to nibble on the chain.

"No," Hannah said, shooing him away. "You ate my last garland. This is the prettiest one I have ever made."

She slipped the garland over her head once more.

After supper, as darkness swept the field, Hannah's father played his flute. She lay back on her bedstraw and counted over one hundred stars.

Suddenly bright light filled the sky.

Hannah blinked. Out of the brilliance, an angel spoke. Hannah only heard part of what the angel said—something about a baby, a sign, a manger, and Bethlehem.

Then more angels filled the air.

They began to sing hallelujahs to God.

After their chorus faded, the night was still and dark again.

"Were those really angels?" Hannah whispered.

"I believe so," her father answered.

"Where is the baby?"

"In a manger in Bethlehem."

"Can we go and see the baby?" Hannah wanted to know.

"Yes, we must," her father said. "The Lord has spoken to us, and Bethlehem is not far. May he protect our sheep while we are gone."

When her father put his arm around her, Hannah could feel that he was shaking. Then she realized that she was shaking too.

The shepherds hurried across the fields

and set out on the road to Bethlehem.

Once in the city, they searched for stables. They found stables with donkeys. They found stables with cows. They found stables with goats and with chickens. Most of the stables had mangers, but they had no baby.

At last, in the distance, they heard a baby cry.

"This way," Hannah pointed.

She ran down the street.

Behind an inn was a stable. Hannah knocked softly, and a man opened the door.

"Here's the sign we are looking for," Hannah called back to her father. "Here is a baby lying in a manger."

"An angel sent us to find your baby," Hannah explained to the man.

"Sir, may we see the child?" her father asked.

The man nodded.

The mother beckoned to Hannah. "Come in and see my baby boy."

Hannah stepped closer. She saw a baby nestled
in sweet-smelling bedstraw. But the flowers of this
bedstraw were not white; they shone like gold.

Hannah touched her garland. Then she slipped it
over her head and handed it to the mother.

"Thank you," the mother said. "You have braided
a lovely garland."

As the mother slipped the garland over her head, Hannah saw the flowers change color.

For a moment, Hannah was too surprised to speak, then she said, "Look! The flowers turned from white to gold. Now they are the same color as your baby's bedstraw."

"This has been a night of miracles," the mother answered.

After a few moments, the mother turned to Hannah. "I am glad you came to see us," she said. "What is your name?"

"Hannah."

"My name is Mary. We will name the baby Jesus."

Hannah's father motioned to her. Before she turned to go,
Hannah touched the tiny hand of baby Jesus.

As Hannah and her father walked back to their sheep, she thought about the wonderful things she had seen.

Hannah thought about the angels in the field and the mother who now wore the garland. She thought about the baby who slept in a manger. And she thought about the miracle that had turned the bedstraw from white to gold.

The next morning Hannah awoke and saw another miracle. In the fields as far as she could see, and in her very own bed, the bedstraw gleamed bright golden in the sun.

All day Hannah braided garland after garland with the gold straw. She looped each one around a cedar tree.

The next year, when the season changed and the fields turned ripe with golden bedstraw, Hannah braided more garlands and hung them around the cedar tree. And she remembered the night of miracles when she touched the hand of baby Jesus who lay in a manger of gold.